8-12

# BLUEBERRY SURPRISE

This Large Print Book carries the
Seal of Approval of N.A.V.H.

# BLUEBERRY SURPRISE

# WANDA E. BRUNSTETTER

**THORNDIKE PRESS**
*A part of Gale, Cengage Learning*

GALE
CENGAGE Learning®

Detroit • New York • San Francisco • New Haven, Conn • Waterville, Maine • London

GALE
CENGAGE Learning

**LIBRARY OF CONGRESS CATALOGING-IN-PUBLICATION DATA**

Brunstetter, Wanda E.
   Blueberry surprise / by Wanda E. Brunstetter. — Large print ed.
      p. cm. — (Love finds a way; #1) (Thorndike Press large print Christian romance)
   ISBN-13: 978-1-4104-4758-6 (hardcover)
   ISBN-10: 1-4104-4758-8 (hardcover)
   1. Large type books. 2. Widows—Fiction. 3. Cooks—Fiction.
I. Title.
PS3602.R864B58 2012
813'.6—dc23                                                    2012001812

Published in 2012 by arrangement with Barbour Publishing, Inc.

Printed in Mexico
3 4 5 6 7 16 15 14 13 12

To my friend Jan Otte,
whose sweet treats
have brought joy
to so many people.
And to my daughter,
Lorine VanCorbach,
a talented musician
who has fulfilled
her heart's desire
of teaching music.

# CHAPTER 1

Rain splattered against the windshield in drops the size of quarters. The darkening sky seemed to swallow Lorna Patterson's compact car as it headed west on the freeway toward the heart of Seattle, Washington.

"I'm sick of this soggy weather," Lorna muttered, gripping the steering wheel with determination and squinting her eyes to see out the filmy window. "I'm drained from working two jobs, and I am not happy with my life."

The burden of weariness crept through Lorna's body, like a poisonous snake about to overtake an unsuspecting victim. Each day as she pulled herself from bed at five in the morning, willing her tired body to move on its own, Lorna asked herself how much longer she could keep going the way she was.

She felt moisture on her cheeks and sniffed deeply. "Will I ever be happy again, Lord? It's been over a year since Ron's death. My heart aches to find joy and meaning in life."

Lorna flicked the blinker switch and turned onto the exit ramp. Soon she was pulling into the parking lot of Farmen's Restaurant, already full of cars.

The place buzzed with activity when she entered through the back door, used only by the restaurant employees and for deliveries. Lorna hung her umbrella and jacket on a wall peg in the coatroom. "I hope I'm not too late," she whispered to her friend and coworker, Chris Williams.

Chris glanced at the clock on the opposite wall. "Your shift was supposed to start half an hour ago, but I've been covering for you."

"Thanks. I appreciate that."

"Is everything all right? You didn't have car troubles, I hope."

Lorna shook her head. "Traffic on the freeway was awful, and the rain didn't make things any easier."

Chris offered Lorna a wide grin, revealing two crescent-shaped dimples set in the middle of her pudgy cheeks. Her light brown hair was pulled up in a ponytail, which made her look less like a woman of thirty-three and more like a teenager. Lorna was glad her own hair was short and naturally curly. She didn't have to do much, other than keep her blond locks clean, trimmed, and combed.

"You know Seattle," Chris said with a snicker. "Weatherwise, it wasn't much of a summer, was it? And now fall is just around the corner."

*It wasn't much of a year either,* Lorna thought ruefully. She drew in a deep breath and released it with a moan. "I am so tired — of everything."

"I'm not surprised." Chris shook her finger. "Work, work, work. That's all you ever do. Clerking at Moore's Mini-Mart during the day and working as a waitress here at night. There's no reason for you to be holding down two jobs now that . . ." She broke off her sentence. "Sorry. It's none of my business how you spend your time. I hate to see you looking so sad and tired, that's all."

Lorna forced a smile. "I know you care, Chris, and I appreciate your concern. You probably don't understand this, but I need to keep busy. It's the only way I can cope with my loss. If I stay active, I don't have time to think or even feel."

"There are other ways to keep busy, you know," Chris reminded her.

"I hope you're not suggesting I start dating again. You know I'm not ready for that." Lorna pursed her lips as she slowly shook her head. "I'm not sure I'll ever be ready to date, much less commit to another man."

"I'm not talking about dating. There

are other things in life besides love and romance. Just ask me — the Old Maid of the West." Chris blinked her eyelids dramatically and wrinkled her nose.

Lorna chuckled, in spite of her dour mood, and donned her red and blue monogrammed Farmen's apron. "What would you suggest I do with my time?"

"How about what you've always wanted to do?"

"And that would be?"

"Follow your heart. Go back to school and get your degree."

Lorna frowned. "Oh, that. I've put my own life on hold so long, I'm not sure I even want college anymore."

"Oh, please!" Chris groaned. "How many times have I heard you complain about having to give up your dream of teaching music to elementary school kids?"

Lorna shrugged. "I don't know. Dozens, maybe."

Chris patted her on the back. "Now's your chance for some real adventure."

Lorna swallowed hard. She knew her friend was probably right, but she also knew going back to school would be expensive, not to mention the fact that she was much older now and would probably feel self-conscious among those college kids. It would be an adventure all right. Most likely a frightening one.

"Think about it," Chris whispered as she headed for the dining room.

"I'll give it some thought," Lorna said to her friend's retreating form.

■ ■ ■ ■

Evan Bailey leaned forward in his chair and studied the recipe that had recently been posted online. "Peanut butter and chocolate chip cookies. Sounds good to me." He figured Cynthia Lyons, his online cooking instructor, must like desserts. Yesterday she'd listed a recipe for peach cobbler, the day before that it was cherries jubilee, and today's sweet treat was his all-time favorite cookie.

Evan was glad he'd stumbled onto the website, especially since learning to cook might fit into his plans for the future.

He hit the PRINT button and smiled. For the past few years he'd been spinning his wheels, not sure whether to make a career of the air force or get out at the end of his tour and go back to college. He was entitled to some money under the GI Bill, so he had finally decided to take advantage of it. Military life had its benefits, but now that Evan was no longer enlisted, he looked forward to becoming a school guidance counselor, or maybe a child psychologist. In a few weeks he would enroll at Bay View Christian College and be on his way to meeting the first of his two goals.

Evan's other goal involved a woman. He had recently celebrated his twenty-eighth birthday and felt ready to settle down. He thought Bay View would offer him not only a good education, but hopefully a sweet, Christian wife as well. He closed his eyes, and visions of a pretty soul mate and a couple of cute kids danced through his head.

Caught up in his musings, Evan hadn't noticed that the paper had jammed in his printer until he opened his eyes again. He reached for the document and gritted his teeth when he saw the blinking light, then snapped open the lid. "I think I might need a new one of these to go along with that wife I'm looking for." He pulled the paper free and chuckled. "Of course, she'd better not be full of wrinkles, like this pitiful piece of paper."

Drawing his gaze back to the computer, Evan noticed on the website that not only was Cynthia Lyons listing one recipe per day, but beginning tomorrow, she would be opening her chat room to anyone interested in discussing the dos and don'ts of making sweet treats. Her note mentioned that the participants would be meeting once a week at six o'clock Pacific standard time.

"Good. It's the same time zone as Seattle. Wonder where she lives?" Evan positioned his cursor over the sign-up list and hit ENTER. Between the recipes Cynthia posted regularly and the online chat, he was sure he'd be cooking up a storm in no time at all.

When Lorna arrived home from work a few minutes before midnight, she found her mother-in-law in the living room, reading a book.

"You're up awfully late," Lorna remarked, taking a seat on the couch beside Ann.

"I was waiting for you," the older woman answered with a smile. "I wanted to talk to you about something."

"Is anything wrong?"

"Everything here is fine. It's you I'm worried about," Ann said, squinting her pale green eyes.

"What do you mean?"

"My son has been dead for over a year, and you're still grieving." A look of concern clouded Ann's face. "You're working two jobs, but there's no reason for it anymore. You have a home here for as long as you like, and Ed and I ask nothing in return." She reached over and gave Lorna's hand a gentle squeeze. "You shouldn't be wearing yourself out for nothing. If you keep going this way, you'll get sick."

Lorna sank her top teeth into her bottom lip so hard she tasted blood. This was the second lecture she'd had in one evening, and she wasn't in the mood to hear it. She loved Ron's parents as if they were her own. She'd chosen to live in their home after his death because she thought it would bring comfort to all three of them. Lorna didn't want hard feelings to come between them, and she certainly didn't want to say or do anything that might offend this lovely, gracious woman.

"Ann, I appreciate your concern," Lorna began, searching for words she hoped wouldn't sound harsh. "I am dealing with Ron's death the best way I can, but I'm not like you. I can't be content to stay home and knit sweaters or crochet lacy tablecloths. I have to keep busy outside the house. It keeps me from getting bored or dwelling on what can't be changed."

"Busy is fine, but you've become a workaholic, and it's not healthy — mentally or physically." Ann adjusted her metal-framed reading glasses so they were sitting correctly on the bridge of her nose. "Ed and I love you, Lorna. We think of you as the daughter we never had. We only want what's best for you." Her short, coffee-colored hair was peppered with gray, and she pushed a stray curl behind her ear.

"I love you both, and I know you have my welfare in mind, but I'm a big girl now, so you needn't worry." Lorna knew her own parents would probably be just as concerned for her well-being if she were living with them. She was almost thankful Mom and Dad lived in Minnesota, because she didn't need two sets of doting parents right now.

"Ed and I don't expect you to give up your whole life for us," Ann continued, as though Lorna hadn't spoken on her own behalf. "You moved from your home state to attend college here; then shortly after you and Ron married, you dropped out of school so you could work and pay his way. Then you kept on working after he entered med school, in order to help pay all the bills for his schooling."

Lorna didn't need to be reminded of the sacrifices she'd made. She was well aware of what she'd given up for the man she loved. "I'm not giving up my life for anyone now," she said as she sighed deeply and pushed against the sofa cushion. Ann didn't understand the way she felt. No one did.

"Have you considered what you might like to do with the rest of your life?" her mother-in-law persisted. "Surely you don't want to spend it working two jobs and holding your middle-aged in-laws' hands."

Lorna blinked back sudden tears that threatened to spill over. She used to think she and Ron would grow old together and have a happy marriage like his parents and hers did. She'd imagined them having children and turning into a real family after he became a physician, but that would never happen now. Lorna had spent the last year worried about helping

Ron's parents deal with their loss, and she'd continued to put her own life on hold.

She swallowed against the lump in her throat. It didn't matter. Her hopes and dreams died the day Ron's body was lowered into that cold, dark grave.

She wrapped her arms around her middle and squeezed her eyes shut. Was it time to stop grieving and follow her heart? Could she do it? Did she even want to anymore?

"I've been thinking," Ann said, breaking into Lorna's troubling thoughts.

"What?"

"When you quit school to help pay our son's way, you were cheated out of the education you deserved. I think you should go back to college and get that music degree you were working toward."

Lorna stirred uneasily. First Chris, and now Ann? What was going on? Was she the victim of some kind of conspiracy? She extended her legs and stretched like a cat. "I'm tired. I think I'll go up to bed."

Before she stood up, Lorna touched her mother-in-law's hand. "I appreciate your suggestion, and I promise to sleep on the idea."

" 'Take delight in the Lord, and he will give you the desires of your heart,' " Ann quoted from the book of Psalms. "God is always full of surprises."

Lorna nodded and headed for the stairs. A short time later, she entered her room and flopped onto the canopy bed with a sigh. She lay there a moment, then turned her head to the right so she could study the picture sitting on the dresser across the room. It was taken on her wedding day, and she and Ron were smiling and looking at each other as though they had their whole lives ahead of them. How happy they'd been back then — full of hope and dreams for their future.

A familiar pang of regret clutched Lorna's heart as she thought about the plans she'd made for her own life. She'd given up her heart's desire in order to help Ron's vision come true. Now they were both gone — Ron, as well as Lorna's plans and dreams.

With the back of her hand, she swiped at an errant tear running down her cheek. *Help me know what to do, Lord. Could You possibly want me to go back to school? Can I really have the desires of my heart? Do You have any pleasant surprises ahead for me?*

# CHAPTER 2

"What did the ground say to the rain?" Lorna asked an elderly man as she waited on his table.

He glanced out the window at the pouring rain and shrugged. "You got me."

"If you keep this up, my name will be mud!" Lorna's laugh sounded forced, but it was the best she could do, considering how hard she'd had to work at telling the dumb joke.

"That was really lame," Chris moaned as she passed by her table and jabbed Lorna in the ribs.

The customer, however, laughed at Lorna's corny quip. She smiled. *Could mean another nice tip.*

She moved to the next table, preparing to take an order from a young couple.

"I'll have one of the greasiest burgers you've got, with a side order of artery-clogging french fries." The man looked up at Lorna and winked.

Offering him what she hoped was a pleasant smile, Lorna wrote down his order. Then she turned to the woman and asked, "What would you like?"

"I'm trying to watch my weight," the slender young woman said. "What have you got that tastes good and isn't full of fat or too many calories?"

"You don't look like you need to worry about your weight at all."

Lorna grinned. "Why, did you know that diets are for people who are thick and tired of it all?"

The woman giggled. "I think I'll settle for a dinner salad and a glass of unsweetened iced tea."

When Lorna turned in her order, she bumped into Chris, who was doing the same.

"What's with you tonight?" her friend asked.

"What do you mean?"

"I've never seen you so friendly to the customers before. And those jokes, Lorna. Where did you dig them up?"

Lorna shrugged. "You're not the only one who can make people laugh, you know. I'll bet my tips will be better than ever tonight."

"Tips? Is that what you're trying to

do — get more tips?"

"Not necessarily more. Just bigger ones." As she spoke the words, Lorna felt a pang of guilt. She knew it wasn't right to try to wangle better tips. The motto at Farmen's was to be friendly and courteous to all customers. Besides, it was the Christian way, and Lorna knew better than to do anything other than that. She'd gotten carried away with the need to make more money in less time. *Forgive me, Father,* she prayed.

Chris moved closer to Lorna. "Let me see if I understand this right. You're single, living rent free with your in-laws, working two jobs, and you need more money? What gives?"

"I've given my notice at the Mini-Mart," Lorna answered. "Next Friday will be my last day."

Chris's mouth dropped open, and she sucked in her breath. "You're kidding!"

"I'm totally serious. I'll only be working at this job from now on."

"You don't even like waiting tables," Chris reminded. "Why would you give up your day job to come here every evening and put up with a cranky boss and complaining customers? If you want to quit a job, why not this one?"

"I decided to take your advice," Lorna replied.

"My advice? Now that's a first. What, might I ask, are you taking my advice on?"

"One week from Monday I'll be registering for the fall semester at Bay View Christian College."

Chris's eyes grew large, and Lorna

gave her friend's red and blue apron a little tug. "Please don't stand there gaping at me — say something."

Chris blinked as though she were coming out of a trance. "I'm in shock. I can't believe you're actually going back to college, much less doing it at my suggestion."

Lorna wrinkled her nose. "It wasn't solely because of your prompting."

"Oh?"

"Ann suggested it the other night, too, and I've been praying about it ever since. I feel it's something I should do."

Chris grabbed Lorna in a bear hug. "I'm so happy for you."

"Thanks." Lorna nodded toward their boss, Gary Farmen, who had just walked by. "Guess we should get back to work."

"Right." Chris giggled. "We wouldn't want to be accused of having any fun on the job, now, would we?"

Lorna started toward the dining room.

"One more thing," Chris called after her.

"What's that?" Lorna asked over her shoulder.

"I'd find some better jokes if I were you."

The distinctive, crisp scent of autumn was in the air. Lorna inhaled deeply as she shuffled through a pile of freshly fallen leaves scattered around the campus of Bay View Christian College.

Today she would register for the fall semester, bringing her one step closer to realizing her dream of teaching music. The decision to return to school had been a difficult one. Certainly she was mature enough to handle the pressures that would come with being a full-time student, but she worried about being too mature to study with a bunch of kids who probably didn't have a clue what life was all about.

By the time Lorna reached the front door of the admissions office, her heart was pounding so hard she was sure everyone within earshot could hear it. Her knees felt weak and shaky, and she wondered if she would be able to hold up long enough to get through this process.

She'd already filled out the necessary paperwork for preadmission and had even met with her adviser the previous week. Today was just a formality. Still, the long line forming behind the desk where she was to pick up her course package made her feel ill at ease.

Lorna fidgeted with the strap of her purse and felt relief wash over her when it was finally her turn.

"Name?" asked the dark-haired, middle-aged woman who was handing out the packets.

"Lorna Patterson. My major is music education."

The woman thumbed through the alphabetized bundles. A few seconds later, she handed one to Lorna. "This is yours."

"Thanks," Lorna mumbled. She turned and began looking through the packet, relieved when she saw that the contents confirmed her schedule for this semester.

Intent on reading the program for her anatomy class, Lorna wasn't watching where she was going. With a sudden jolt, she bumped into someone's arm, and the entire bundle flew out of her hands. Feeling a rush of heat creep up the back of her neck, Lorna dropped to her knees to retrieve the scattered papers.

"Sorry. Guess my big bony elbow must have gotten in your way. Here, let me help you with those."

Lorna looked up. A pair of clear blue eyes seemed to be smiling at her. The man those mesmerizing eyes belonged to must be the owner of the deep voice offering help. She fumbled with the uncooperative papers, willing her fingers to stop shaking. *What is wrong with me? I'm acting like a clumsy fool this morning.* "Thanks, but I can manage," she squeaked.

The young man nodded as he got to his feet, and her cheeks burned hot under his scrutiny.

Lorna quickly gathered up the remaining papers and stood. *He probably thinks I'm a real klutz. So much for starting out the day on the right foot.*

The man opened his mouth as if to say something, but Lorna hurried away. She still had to go to the business office and take care of some financial matters. Then she needed to find the bookstore and locate whatever she'd be needing, and finally the student identification desk to get her ID card. There would probably be long lines everywhere.

Lorna made her way down the crowded hall, wondering how many more stupid blunders she might make before the day was over. She'd been away from college so long; it was obvious she no longer knew how to function. Especially in the presence of a good-looking man.

Evan hung his bicycle on the rack outside his lake-view apartment building and bounded up the steps, feeling rather pleased with himself. He'd enrolled at Bay View Christian College today, taken a leisurely bike ride around Woodland Park, and now was anxious to get home and grab a bite to eat. After supper he'd be going online to check out Cynthia Lyons's cooking class again. Maybe he'd have better luck with today's recipe than he had last week. Evan's peanut butter chocolate chip cookies turned out hard as rocks, and he still hadn't figured out what he'd done wrong. He thought he'd followed Cynthia's directions to the letter, but apparently he'd left out some important ingredient. He probably should try making them again.

As soon as Evan entered his apartment, he went straight to the kitchen and pulled a dinner from the freezer, then popped it into the oven.

"If I learn how to cook halfway decent, it might help find me a wife," he murmured. "Not only that, but it would mean I'd be eating better meals while I wait for that special someone."

While the frozen dinner heated, Evan went to the living room, where his computer sat on a desk in the corner. He booted it up, then went back to the kitchen to fix a salad. At least that was something he could do fairly well.

"I should have insisted Mom teach me how to cook," he muttered.

As Evan prepared the green salad, his thoughts turned toward home. He'd grown up in Moscow, Idaho, and that's where his parents and two older sisters still lived with their families. Since Evan was the youngest child and the only boy in the family, he'd never really needed to cook. His sisters, Margaret and Ellen, had always helped Mom in the kitchen, and they used to say Evan was just in the way if he tried to help out. So when Evan went off to college, he lived on fast food and meals that were served in the school's cafeteria. When he dropped out of college to join the air force, all of his meals were provided, so again he had no reason to cook.

Now Evan was living in Seattle, attending the Christian college a friend had recommended. He probably could have lived on campus and eaten whatever was available, but he'd chosen to live alone and learn to cook. He'd also decided it was time to settle down and look for a Christian woman.

Evan sliced a tomato and dropped the pieces into the salad bowl. "First order of business — learn to cook. Second order — find a wife!"

Over the last few days, Lorna's tips from the restaurant had increased, and she figured it might have something to do with the fact that she'd given up telling jokes and was being pleasant and friendly, without any ulterior motives.

"I see it's raining again," Chris said as she stepped up beside Lorna.

Lorna grabbed her work apron and shrugged. "What else is new? We're living in Washington — the Evergreen State, remember?"

Chris lifted her elbow, let it bounce a few times, then connected it gently to Lorna's rib cage. "You're not planning to tell that silly joke about the ground talking to the rain again, I hope."

Lorna shook her head. "I've decided to stick to business and leave the humorous stuff to real people like you."

Chris raised her dark eyebrows, giving Lorna a quizzical look. "*Real* people? What's that supposed to mean?"

"It means you're fun-loving and genuinely witty." Lorna frowned. "You don't have to tell stale jokes in order to make people smile. Everyone seems drawn to your pleasant personality."

"Thanks for the compliment," Chris said with a nod. "I think you sell yourself short. You're talented, have gorgeous, curly blond hair, and you're blessed with a genuine, sweet spirit." She leaned closer and whispered, "Trouble is, you keep it hidden, like a dark secret you don't want anyone to discover."

Lorna moved away, hoping to avoid any more of her friend's psychoanalyzing, but Chris stepped in front of her, planting both hands on her wide hips. "I'm not done yet."

Lorna squinted her eyes. "It's obvious that you're not going to let me go to work until I hear you out."

Chris's smile was a victorious one. "If you would learn to relax and quit taking life so seriously, people would be drawn to you."

Lorna groaned. "I want to, Chris, but since Ron's death, life has so little meaning for me."

"You're still young and have lots to offer the world. Don't let your heart stay locked up in a self-made prison."

"Maybe going back to school will help. Being around kids who are brimming over with enthusiasm and still believe life holds nothing but joy might rub off on me."

"I think most college kids are smart enough to know life isn't always fun and games," Chris said in a serious tone. "I do believe you're right about one thing though."

"What's that?"

"Going back to school will be good for you."

# CHAPTER 3

Lorna settled herself into one of the hard-backed auditorium seats and pulled a notebook and pen from her backpack. Anatomy was her first class of the day. She wanted to be ready for action, since this course had been suggested by one of the advisers. It would help her gain a better understanding of proper breathing and the body positions involved in singing.

She glanced around, noticing about fifty other students in the room. Most of them were also preparing to take notes.

A tall, middle-aged man, who introduced himself as Professor Talcot, announced the topic of the day —
"Age-Related Changes."

Lorna was about to place her backpack on the empty seat next to her
when someone sat down. She glanced
over and was greeted with a friendly
smile.

*Oh no! It's that guy I bumped into the
other day during registration.*

She forced a return smile, then
quickly averted her attention back to
the professor.

"I'm late. Did I miss much?" the
man whispered as he leaned toward
Lorna.

"He just started." She kept her gaze
straight ahead.

"Okay, thanks."

Lorna was grateful he didn't say

anything more. She was here to learn, not to be distracted by some big kid who should have been on time for his first class of the day.

"Everyone, take a good look at the seat you're in," Professor Talcot said. "That's where you will sit for the remainder of the semester. My assistant will be around shortly to get your names and fill out the seating chart."

Lorna groaned inwardly. If she'd known she would have to stay in this particular seat all semester, she might have been a bit more selective. Of course, she had no way of knowing an attractive guy with gorgeous blue eyes and a winning smile was going to flop into the seat beside her.

*I can handle this. After all, it's only one hour a day. I don't even have to talk to him if I don't want to.*

"Name, please?"

Lorna was jolted from her thoughts when a studious-looking man wearing metal-framed glasses tapped her on the shoulder.

She turned her head and realized he was standing in the row behind, leaning slightly over the back of her seat, holding a clipboard in one hand.

"Lorna Patterson," she whispered.

"What was that? I couldn't hear you."

The man sitting next to Lorna turned around. "She said her name is Lorna Patterson. Mine's Evan Bailey."

"Gotcha!" the aide replied.

Lorna felt the heat of embarrassment rush to her cheeks. *Great! He not only saw how clumsy I was the other day; now he thinks I can't even speak for myself. I must appear to be pretty stupid.*

As she turned her attention back to the class, Lorna caught the tail end of something the professor had said. Something about a group of five. *That's what I get for thinking when I should be listening. Maybe I wasn't ready to come back to college after all.* She turned to Evan and reluctantly asked, "What did the professor say?"

"He said he's about to give us our first assignment, and we're supposed to form into groups of five." A smile tugged at the corners of his mouth. "Would you like to be in my group?"

Lorna shrugged. She didn't know anyone else in the class. Not that she knew Evan. She'd only met him once, and that wasn't under the best of circumstances.

Evan Bailey was obviously more outgoing than she, for he was already rounding up three other people to join their group — two young men and one woman, all sitting in the row ahead of them.

"The first part of this assignment will be to get to know each other," Professor Talcot told the class. "Tell everyone in your group your name, age, and major."

Lorna felt a sense of dread roll over her, like turbulent breakers lapping against the shore.

*It's bad enough that I'm older than most of these college kids. Is it really necessary for me to reveal my age?*

Introductions were quickly made, and Lorna soon learned the others in the group were Jared, Tim, and

Vanessa. All but Evan and Lorna had given some information about themselves.

"You want to go first?" Evan asked, looking at Lorna.

"I — uh — am in my junior year, and I'm majoring in music ed. I hope to become an elementary school music teacher when I graduate."

"Sounds good. How about you, Evan?" Tim, the studious-looking one, asked.

Evan wiggled his eyebrows and gave Lorna a silly grin. "I'm lookin' for a mother for my children."

"You have kids?" The question came from Vanessa, who had long red hair and dark brown eyes, which she'd kept focused on Evan ever since they'd formed their group.

He shook his head. "Nope, not yet.

I'm still searching for the right woman to be my wife. I need someone who loves the Lord as much as I do." Evan's eyebrows drew together. "Oh yeah — it might be good if she knows how to cook. I'm in the process of learning, but so far all my recipes have flopped."

Vanessa leaned forward and studied Evan more intently. "Are you majoring in home economics?"

Evan chuckled. "Not even close. My major is psychology, but I've recently signed up for an online cooking class." He smiled and nodded at Lorna instead of Vanessa. "You married?"

Lorna shook her head. "I'm not married now." She hesitated then looked away. "My husband died."

"Sorry to hear that," Evan said in a

sincere tone.

"Yeah, it's a shame about your husband," Jared agreed.

There were a few moments of uncomfortable silence; then Evan said, "I thought I might bring some sweet treats to class one of these days and share them with anyone willing to be my guinea pig."

Vanessa smacked her lips and touched the edge of Evan's shirtsleeve. "I'll be looking forward to that."

"It's time to tell our ages. I'm twenty-one," Tim said.

Vanessa smiled and said she was also twenty-one.

Jared informed the group that he was twenty-four.

"Guess that makes me the old man of our little assemblage. I'm heading downhill at the ripe old age of twenty-eight," Evan said with a wink in Lorna's direction.

*With the exception of Evan, they're all just kids,* she thought. *And even he's four years younger than me.*

Vanessa nudged Lorna's arm with the eraser end of her pencil. "Now it's your turn."

Lorna stared at the floor and mumbled, "I'm thirty-two."

Jared let out a low whistle. "Wow, you're a lot older than the rest of us."

Lorna slid a little lower in her chair. *As if I needed to be reminded.*

Evan held up the paper he was holding. It had been handed out by the professor's assistant only moments ago. "It says here that one of the most significant age-related signs is increased hair growth in the nose."

He leaned over until his face was a few inches from Lorna's. As he studied her, she felt like a bug under a microscope. "Yep," he announced. "I can see it's happening to you already!"

Jared, Tim, and Vanessa howled, and Lorna covered her face with her hands. If the aisle hadn't been blocked, she might have dashed for the door. Instead, she drew in a deep breath, lifted her head, and looked Evan in the eye. "You're right about my nose hair. In fact, I'm so old I get winded just playing a game of checkers." She couldn't believe she'd said that. Maybe those stupid jokes she had used on her customers at the restaurant were still lodged in her brain.

Everyone in the group laughed this

time, including Lorna, who was finally beginning to relax. "The other day, I sank my teeth into a big, juicy steak, and you know what?" she quipped.

Evan leaned a bit closer. "What?"

"They just stayed there!"

Vanessa giggled and poked Evan on the arm. "She really got you good on that one."

Evan grimaced. "Guess I deserved it. Sorry about the nose hair crack."

He looked genuinely sorry, making Lorna feel foolish for trying to set him up with her lame joke. She was about to offer an apology of her own when he added, "It's nice to know I'm not the oldest one in class."

Lorna didn't know how she had survived the morning. By the time she entered her last class of the day, she wondered all the more if she was going to make it as a college student. *This is no time to wimp out,* she chided herself as she took a seat in the front row. *Choir is my favorite subject.*

The woman who stood in front of the class introduced herself as Professor Lynne Burrows.

*She's young,* Lorna noted. *Probably not much past thirty. I would be a music teacher by now if I'd finished my studies ten years ago.*

"Do we have any pianists in this class?" Professor Burrows asked.

Lorna glanced around the room. When she saw no hands raised, she lifted hers.

"Have you ever accompanied a choir?"

She nodded. "I play for my church

choir, and I also accompanied college choir during my freshman and sophomore years." She chose not to mention the fact that it had been several years ago.

The professor smiled. "Would you mind playing for us today? If it works out well, perhaps you'd consider doing it for all the numbers that require piano accompaniment."

"I'd like that." Lorna headed straight for the piano, a place where she knew she'd be the most comfortable.

"If you need someone to turn the pages, I'd be happy to oblige."

Lorna glanced to her right. Evan Bailey was leaning on the lid of the piano, grinning at her like a monkey who'd been handed a tasty banana. She couldn't believe he was in her music class, too.

"Thanks anyway, but I think I can manage," Lorna murmured.

Evan dropped to the bench beside her. "I've done this before, and I'm actually pretty good at it." He reached across Lorna and thumbed a few pages of the music.

She eyed him suspiciously. "You don't know when to quit, do you?"

He laughed and wagged a finger in front of her nose. "Just call me Pushy Bailey."

"Let's see what Professor Burrows has to say when she realizes you're sitting on the piano bench instead of standing on the risers with the rest of the choir. You *are* enrolled in this class, I presume?"

Evan smiled at her. "I am, and I signed up for it just so I could perfect my talent of page turning."

Lorna moaned softly. "You're impossible."

Evan dragged his fingers along the piano keys. "How about you and me going out for a burger after class? Then I can tell you about the rest of my faults."

"Sorry, but I don't date."

He snapped the key of middle C up and down a few times. "Who said anything about a date? I'm hungry for a burger and thought maybe you'd like to join me. It would be a good chance for us to get better acquainted."

Lorna sucked in her breath. "Why would we need to get better acquainted?"

He gave her a wide smile. "I'm in choir — you're in choir. You're the pianist — I'm the page turner. I'm in anatomy — you're in anatomy. I'm in your group — you're in my —"

She held up one hand. "Okay, Mr. Bailey. I get the point."

"Call me Evan. Mr. Bailey makes me sound like an old man."

"Evan, then."

"So will you have a burger with me?"

Lorna opened her mouth, but Professor Burrows leaned on top of the piano and spoke first. "I see you've already found a page turner."

Lorna shook her head. "Not really. I've always been able to turn my own pages, and I'm sure you need Mr. Bailey's voice in the tenor section far more than I need his thumb and index finger at the piano."

Evan grinned up at the teacher.

"What can I say? The woman likes me."

Lorna's mouth dropped open. Didn't the guy ever quit?

"You're pretty self-confident, aren't you?" The professor pointed at Evan, then motioned toward the risers. "Let's see how well you can sing. Third row, second place on the left."

Evan shrugged and gave Lorna a quick wink. "See you later."

"Don't mind him," Professor Burrows whispered to Lorna. "I think he's just testing the waters."

"Mine or yours?"

"Probably both. I've handled characters like him before, so we won't let it get out of hand." The professor gave Lorna's shoulder a gentle squeeze and moved to the front of the class.

Lorna closed her eyes and drew in a deep breath, lifting a prayer of thanks that the day was almost over. She couldn't believe how stressful it had been. Maybe she should give up her dream of becoming a music teacher while she still had some shred of sanity left.

As Evan stood on the risers with the rest of the class, he couldn't keep focused on Professor Burrows or the song they were supposed to be singing. His gaze kept going back to the cute little blond who sat at the piano.

He knew Lorna was four years older than he, and she'd made it clear that she had no interest in dating. Still, the woman fascinated him, and he was determined they should get better acquainted. The few years' age difference meant nothing as far as he was concerned, but it might matter to Lorna. Maybe that's why she seemed so indifferent.

*I'd sure like to get to know her better and find out if we're compatible.* Evan smiled to himself. He would figure out a way — maybe bribe her with one of his online sweet treats. Of course, he'd first have to learn how to bake something that didn't flop.

# CHAPTER 4

When Lorna arrived home from school, she found her father-in-law in the front yard, raking a pile of maple leaves into a mountain in the middle of the lawn.

Ed stopped and wiped the perspiration from the top of his bald head with a hankie he had pulled from the pocket of his jeans. "How was your first day?"

Lorna plodded up the steps, dropped her backpack to the porch, and sank wearily into one of the wicker chairs. "Let's put it this way:

I'm still alive to tell about it."

Ed leaned the rake against the outside porch railing and took the chair beside her. "That bad, huh?"

She only nodded in reply.

"Is your schedule too heavy this semester?" he asked, obvious concern revealed in his dark eyes.

Lorna forced a smile. "It's nothing to be worried about."

"Anything that concerns you concerns me and Ann. You were married to our son, and that makes us family."

"I know, but I do have to learn how to handle some problems on my own."

"Problems? Did I hear someone say they're having problems?"

Lorna glanced up at Ann, who had stepped onto the porch. "It's nothing. I'm just having a hard time fitting in at school. I am quite a bit older than most of my classmates, you know."

Ann laughed, causing the lines around her eyes to become more pronounced. "Is that all that's troubling you? I'd think being older would have some advantages."

"Such as?"

"For one thing, your maturity should help you grasp things. Your study habits will probably be better than those of most kids fresh out of high school, too. These days, many young people don't have a lot of self-discipline."

"Yeah, no silly schoolgirl crushes or other such distractions," Ed put in with a deep chuckle.

Lorna swallowed hard. There had

already been plenty of distractions today, and they'd come in the form of a young man with laughing blue eyes, goofy jokes, and a highly contagious smile.

"My maturity might help me be more studious, but it sure sets me apart from the rest of the college crowd," she said. "Today I felt like a sore thumb sticking out on an otherwise healthy hand."

"You're so pretty, I'm sure no one even guessed you were a few years older." Ann gently touched Lorna's shoulder.

"Thanks for the compliment," Lorna said, making no mention of the fact that she had already revealed her age during the first class of the day. She cringed, thinking about the nose hair incident. "I'd better go inside. I want to read a few verses of scripture, and I have some homework that needs to be done before it's time to head for work."

Lorna stood in front of the customer who sat at a table in her assigned section with a menu in front of his face. "Have you decided yet, sir?" she asked.

"I'll have a cheeseburger with the works."

He dropped the menu to the table, and Lorna's gaze darted to the man's face. "Wh–what are you doing here?" she rasped.

Evan smiled up at her. "I'm ordering a hamburger, and seeing you again makes me remember that you stood me up this afternoon."

"How could I have stood you up

when I never agreed to go out with you in the first place?" Lorna's hands began to tremble, and she knew her cheeks must be pink, because she could feel the heat quickly spreading.

Evan's grin widened. "You never really said no."

Lorna clenched her pencil in one hand and the order pad in the other. "Did you follow me here from my home?"

"I don't even know where you live, so how could I have followed you?" Evan studied his menu again. "I think I'll have an order of fries to go with that burger. Care to join me?"

"In case you hadn't noticed, I'm working."

"Hmm . . . Maybe I'll have a chocolate shake, too."

Lorna tapped her foot impatiently.

"How did you know I worked here?"

He handed her the menu. "I didn't. I've heard this restaurant serves really great burgers, and I thought I'd give it a try. The fact that you work here is just an added bonus."

"I'll be back when your order is up." Lorna turned on her heels and headed for the kitchen, but she'd only made it halfway when she collided with Chris. Apple pie, vanilla ice cream, and two chocolate-covered donuts went sailing through the air as her friend's tray flew out of her hands.

Lorna gasped. "Oh Chris, I'm so sorry! I didn't see you coming."

"It was just an accident. It's okay — I know you didn't do it on purpose," Chris said as she dropped to her knees.

Lorna did the same and quickly began to help clean up the mess. "I'll probably be docked half my pay for this little blunder," she grumbled. "I ought to send Evan Bailey a bill."

Chris's eyebrows shot up. "Who's Evan Bailey?"

"Some guy I met at school. I have him in two of my classes. He's here tonight. I just took his order."

Chris gave her a quizzical look. "And?"

"He had me so riled I wasn't paying attention to where I was going." Lorna scooped up the last piece of pie and handed the tray back to Chris. "I really am sorry about this."

Chris laughed. "It's a good thing it went on the floor and not in someone's lap." She got to her feet. "So what's this guy done that has you so upset?"

Lorna picked a hunk of chocolate off her apron and stood, too. "First of all, he kept teasing me in anatomy class this morning. Then he plunked himself down at the piano with me during choir, offering to be my page turner." She paused and drew in a deep breath. "Next, he asked me to go out for a burger after school."

"What'd you say?"

"I didn't answer him." Lorna frowned. "Now he's here, pestering me to eat dinner with him."

Chris moved toward the kitchen, with Lorna following on her heels. "Sounds to me like the guy is interested in you."

Lorna shook her head. "He hardly even knows me. Besides, I'm four years older."

"Who's hung up on age differences nowadays?"

"Okay, it's not the four years between us that really bothers me."

"What, then?"

"He acts like a big kid!" Lorna shrugged. "Besides, even if I was planning to date, which I'm not, our personalities don't mesh."

Evan leaned his elbows on the table and studied the checkered place mat in front of him. He had always been the kind of person who knew what he wanted and then went after it. How come his determination wasn't working this time? *Lorna doesn't believe me. She thinks I've been spying on her and came here to harass her. I've got to make her believe my coming to Farmen's was purely coinci-*

*dental.* He took a sip of water. *Although it could have been an answer to prayer. Somehow I've got to get Lorna to agree to go out with me. How else am I going to know if she's the one?*

A short time later, Lorna returned with Evan's order, and he felt ready to try again. He looked up at her and smiled. "You look cute in that uniform." When she made no comment, he added, "Been working here long?"

"Sometimes it feels like forever," she said with a deep sigh.

"Want to talk about it?"

She shook her head. "Will there be anything else?"

He rapped the edge of the plate with his knife handle. "Actually, there is."

"What can I get for you?"

"How about a few minutes of your time?"

"I'm working."

"When do you get off work? I can stick around for a while."

"Late. I'll be working late tonight."

Evan cringed. He wasn't getting anywhere with this woman and knew he should probably quit while he was ahead. Of course, he wasn't really ahead, so he decided he might as well stick his neck out a little farther. "I'm not trying to come on to you. I just want to get to know you better."

"Why?"

Evan reached for his glass of water and took a sip. How could he explain his attraction to Lorna without scaring her off? "I think we have a lot in common," he said with a nod.

She raised one pale eyebrow. "How

did you reach that conclusion?"

"It's simple. I'm in choir — you're in choir. You're the pianist — I'm the page turner."

"I'm not interested in dating you or anyone else."

Evan grabbed his burger off the plate. "Okay, I get the message. I'll try not to bother you again."

She touched his shoulder unexpectedly, sending a shock wave through his arm. "I–I'm sorry if I came across harshly. I just needed you to know where I stand."

He swallowed the bite of burger he'd put in his mouth. "Are you seeing someone else? You mentioned in class that you're a widow, so I kinda figured —"

Lorna shook her head, interrupting his sentence. "I'm a widow who doesn't date."

Evan thought she looked sad, or maybe she was lonely. He grabbed the bottle of ketchup in the center of the table and smiled at her. "Can we at least be friends?"

She nodded and held out her hand. "Friends."

# CHAPTER 5

Lorna awoke with a headache. She had been back in college a week, and things weren't getting any easier. It was hard to attend school all day, work every evening at Farmen's, and find time to get her assignments finished. She was tired and irritable but knew she would have to put on a happy face when she was at work, no matter how aggravating some of the customers could be. One patron in particular was especially unnerving. Evan Bailey had returned to the restaurant two more times. She wasn't sure if he came because he liked the food, or if it was merely to get under her skin.

Lorna uttered a quick prayer and forced her unwilling body to get out of bed. She couldn't miss any classes today. There was a test to take in English lit and auditions for lead parts in the choir's first performance.

She entered the bathroom and turned on the faucet at the sink. Splashing a handful of water against her upturned face, she cringed as the icy liquid stung her cheeks. Apparently Ann was washing clothes this morning, for there was no hot water.

"Ed needs to get that old tank replaced," Lorna grumbled as she reached for a towel. "Maybe I should stay home today after all."

The verse she'd read the night

before in Psalm 125 popped into her mind. *"Those who trust in the Lord are like Mount Zion, which cannot be shaken but endures forever."*

"Thanks for that reminder, Lord. I need to trust You to help me through this day."

"I don't see how we're ever gonna get better acquainted if you keep avoiding me."

Lorna sat in her anatomy class, watching a video presentation on the muscular system and trying to ignore Evan, who sat on her left. She kept her eyes focused on the video screen. *Maybe if I pretend I didn't hear him, he'll quit pestering me.*

"Here, I brought you something." He leaned closer and held out two cookies encased in plastic wrap.

Lorna could feel his warm breath on her ear, and she shivered.

"You cold?"

When she made no reply and didn't reach for the cookies, he tapped her lightly on the arm. "I made these last night. Please try one."

Lorna didn't want to appear rude, but she wasn't hungry. "I just ate breakfast not long ago."

"That's okay. You can save them for later."

"All right. Thanks." Lorna took the cookies and placed them inside her backpack.

"I'm going biking on Saturday. Do you ride?" he asked.

"Huh?"

"I'd like you to go out with me this Saturday. We can rent some bikes at the park and pedal our way around the lake."

"I told you . . . I don't date."

"I know, but the other night you said we could be friends, so we won't call this a date. It'll just be two lonely people out having a good time."

Lorna's face heated up. "What makes you think I'm lonely?"

"I see it in your eyes," he whispered. "They're sad and lonely looking." When she made no reply, he added, "Look, if you'd rather not go, then —"

Lorna blew out her breath as she threw caution to the wind. "All right, I'll go, but you're taking an awfully big chance."

"Yeah, I know." He snickered. "A few hours spent in your company, and I might never be the same."

Lorna held back the laughter threatening to bubble over, but she couldn't hide her smile. "I was thinking more along the lines of our fall weather. It can be pretty unpredictable this time of the year."

Evan chuckled. "Yeah, like some blond-haired, blue-eyed woman I'd like to get to know a whole lot better."

Evan studied the computer screen intently. Brownie Delight was the sweet treat Cynthia Lyons had posted on Tuesday, but he hadn't had time to check it out until today. The ingredients were basic — unsweetened chocolate, butter, sour cream, sugar, eggs, flour, baking powder, salt, and chopped nuts. Chocolate chips would be sprinkled on top, making it doubly delicious. If the brownies turned out halfway decent, he would take some on his date with Lorna. Maybe she'd be impressed with his ability to cook. He hoped so, because so far nothing he'd said or done had seemed to make an impact on her. She hadn't even said whether she'd liked the chocolate peanut butter cookies he'd given her the other day. Lorna was probably too polite to mention that they'd been a bit overdone. This was Evan's second time with these cookies, and he was beginning to wonder if he'd ever get it right.

Evan still hadn't made it to any of the online chats Cynthia Lyons hosted. Now that he was in school all day, his evenings were usually spent doing homework.

Oh well. The chats were probably just a bunch of chitchat about how well the recipes had turned out for others who had made them. He didn't need any further reminders that his hadn't been so successful.

Evan hit the PRINT button to make a copy of the recipe and leaned back in his chair while he waited for the procedure to complete itself.

A vision of Lorna's petite face flashed into his mind. He was attracted to her; there was no question about that. But did they really have anything in common? Was she someone who wanted to serve the Lord with her whole heart, the way Evan did?

The college they attended was a Christian one, but he knew not everyone who went there was a believer in Christ. Some merely signed up at Bay View because of its excellent academic program. Evan hoped Lorna wasn't one of those.

And what about children? Did she like kids as much as he did? Other than becoming an elementary school music teacher, what were her goals and dreams for the future? He needed to know all these things if he planned to pursue a relationship with her.

The printer had stopped, and Evan grabbed hold of the recipe for Brownie Delight. "Tomorrow Lorna and I will get better acquainted as we pedal around the lake and munch on these sweet treats. Tonight I'll pray about it."

The week had seemed to fly by, and when Lorna awoke Saturday morning, she was in a state of panic. She couldn't believe she'd agreed to go biking with Evan today. What had she been thinking? Up until now, she'd kept him at arm's length, but going on what he probably saw as a date could be a huge mistake.

"Then again," she mumbled, "it might be just the thing to prove to Evan how wrong we are for each other."

Lorna crawled out of bed, wondering what she should wear and what to tell her in-laws at breakfast. Not wanting to raise any questions from Ann or Ed, she decided to tell them only that she'd be going out sometime after lunch, but she would make no mention of where. Her plans were to meet Evan at the park near the college, but she didn't want them to know about it. They might think it was a real date and that she was being untrue to their son's memory. She only hoped by the end of the day she wouldn't regret her decision to spend time alone with Evan Bailey.

At two o'clock that afternoon, Lorna drove into the park. The weather was overcast and a bit chilly, but at least it wasn't raining. She found Evan waiting on a wooden bench, with two bikes parked nearby.

"Hey! I'm glad you came!"

"I said I would."

"I know, but I was afraid you might back out."

Lorna flopped down beside him, and he grinned at her. "You look great today."

She glanced down at her blue jeans and white T-shirt, mostly hidden by a jean jacket, and shrugged. "Nothing fancy, but at least I'm comfortable."

Evan slapped the knees of his faded jeans and tweaked the collar on his black leather jacket. "Yeah, me, too."

A young couple pushing a baby in a stroller walked past, and Lorna stared at them longingly.

"You like kids?"

"What?" She jerked her head.

"I asked if you like kids."

"Sure, they're great."

"When I get married, I'd like to have a whole house full of children," Evan said. "With kids around, it would be a lot harder to grow old and crotchety."

"Like me, you mean?"

Evan reached out to touch her hand. "I didn't mean that at all."

She blinked in rapid succession. "I am a lot older than most of the other students at Bay View."

"You're not much older than me. When I was born, you were only four."

She grunted. "When you were six, I was ten."

"When you were twenty-six, I was twenty-two." Evan nudged her arm with his elbow. "I'm gaining on you, huh?"

Lorna jumped up and grabbed the women's ten-speed by the handlebars. "I thought we came here to ride bikes, not talk about age-related things."

Evan stood, too. "You're right, so you lead — I'll follow."

They rode in pleasant silence, Lorna leading and Evan bringing up the rear. They were nearly halfway around the park when he pedaled alongside her. "You hungry? I brought along a few apples and some brownies I made last night."

She pulled her bicycle to a stop. "That does sound good. I haven't ridden a bike in years, and I'm really out of shape. A little rest and some nourishment might help get me going again."

Evan led them to a picnic table, set his kickstand, and motioned her to take a seat. When they were both seated, he reached into his backpack and withdrew two Red Delicious apples, then handed one to Lorna. "Let's eat these first and save the brownies for dessert."

"Thanks." Lorna bit into hers, and a trickle of sweet, sticky juice dribbled down her chin. "Mmm . . . this does hit the spot." She looked over at him and smiled. "Sorry about being such a grump earlier. Guess I'm a little touchy about my age."

"Apology accepted. Uh . . . would you like to go to dinner when we're done riding?" Evan asked hesitantly.

Warning bells went off in Lorna's head, and she felt her whole body tremble. "I'm not dressed for going out."

"I was thinking about pizza. We don't have to be dressed up for that." Evan bit into his apple and grinned.

That dopey little smile and the gentleness in his eyes made Lorna's heartbeat quicken. She gulped. "I — I —"

"You can think about it while we finish our ride," Evan said, coming to her rescue.

She shrugged her shoulders.

"Okay."

"So, tell me about Lorna Patterson."

"What do you want to know?"

"I know you're enrolled in a Christian college. Does that mean you're a believer in Christ?"

She nodded. "I accepted the Lord as my personal Savior when I was ten years old. At that time I thought I knew exactly what He wanted me to do with my life."

"Which was?"

"To teach music. I started playing piano right around the time I became a Christian, and I soon discovered that I loved it."

"You're definitely a gifted pianist," he said with a broad smile. "You do great accompanying our choir, and you have a beautiful singing voice."

"Thanks." She nodded at him. "Is that all you wanted to know about me?"

"Actually, there is something else I've been wondering about."

"What?"

"You mentioned that you're a widow. How did your husband die?"

Lorna stared off into the distance, focusing on a cluster of pigeons eating dry bread crumbs someone had dumped on the grass. She didn't want to talk about Ron, her loss, or how he'd been killed so tragically.

"If you'd rather not discuss it, that's okay." Evan touched her arm gently. "I probably shouldn't have asked, but I want to know you better, so —"

Lorna turned her head so she was looking directly at him. "It's okay. It'll probably do me more good to talk about it than it will to keep it bottled up." She drew in a deep breath and plunged ahead. "Ron was killed in a motorcycle accident a little over a year ago. A semitruck hit him."

"I'm so sorry. It must have been hard for you."

"It was. Still is, in fact."

"Have you been on your own ever since?"

She shook her head. "Not exactly. I've been living with Ron's parents, hoping it would help the three of us deal with our grief."

"And has it?"

"Some."

Compassion showed in Evan's eyes, and he took hold of her hand. It felt warm and comforting, and even though Lorna's head told her to pull away, her heart said something entirely different. So she sat there, staring down at their intertwined fingers and basking in the moment of comfort and pleasure.

"I'm surprised a woman your age, who's blessed with lots of talent and good looks, hasn't found another man by now."

Lorna felt her face flame. She focused on the apple core in her other hand, already turning brown. When she spotted a garbage can a few feet away, Lorna stood up. Before she could take a step, she felt Evan's hand on her arm.

"I'm sorry, Lorna. I can tell I've upset you. Was it my question about your husband's death, or was it the fact that I said I was surprised you hadn't found another man?"

She blinked away unwanted tears.

"A little of both, I suppose."

She stiffened as Evan's arm went around her shoulders. "Still friends?"

"Sure," she mumbled.

"Does that mean you'll have pizza with me?"

"I thought I had until the bike ride was over to decide."

He twitched his eyebrows. "What can I say? I'm not the patient type."

"No, but you're certainly persistent."

He handed her a napkin and two brownies. "How do you think I've gotten this far in life?"

She sucked in her breath. How far had he gotten? Other than the fact that he was majoring in psychology, wasn't married, and was four years younger than she, Lorna knew practically nothing about Evan Bailey.

Maybe she should learn more — in case she needed another friend.

She tossed the apple core into the garbage and bit into one of the brownies. "Where'd you say you got these?"

"Made them myself. I think I already told you that I'm taking an online cooking class. Right now the instructor is teaching us how to make some tasty sweet treats." He winked at her. "I thought it might make me a better catch if I could cook."

Lorna wasn't sure what to say. She didn't want to hurt Evan's feelings by telling him the brownie was too dry. She thought about the cookies he'd given her the other day. She'd tried one at lunch, and they had been equally dry, not to mention a bit overdone. Apparently the man was so new at cooking, he couldn't tell that much himself. She ate the brownie in silence and washed it down with the bottled water Evan had also supplied. When she was done, Lorna climbed onto her bike. "We'd better go. I hear the best pizza in town is at Mama Mia's!"

# CHAPTER 6

Lorna slid into a booth at the pizza parlor, and Evan took the bench across from her. When their waitress came, they ordered a large combination pizza and a pitcher of iced tea.

As soon as the server was gone, Evan leaned forward on his elbows and gave Lorna a crooked smile. "You're beautiful, you know that?"

She gulped. No one but Ron had ever looked at her as if she were the most desirable woman on earth. Lorna leaned back in her seat and slid her tongue across her bottom lip.

"Now it's your turn to tell me about Evan Bailey," she said, hoping the change in subject might calm her racing heart and get her thinking straight again.

She watched the flame flicker from the candle in the center of the table and saw its reflection in Evan's blue eyes. "My life is an open book, so what would you like to know?" he asked.

*I'd like to know why you're looking at me like that.* "You told our group in class that your major is psychology, but you never said what you plan to do with it once you graduate," she said, instead of voicing her thoughts.

The waitress brought two glasses and a pitcher of iced tea to the table. As soon as she left, Evan poured them both a glass. "I'm hoping to land a job as a school guidance counselor, but if that doesn't work out, I might go into private practice as a child psychologist."

Lorna peered at him over the top of her glass. "Let me guess. I'll bet you plan to analyze kids all day and then come home at night to the little woman who's been busy taking care of your own children. Is that right?"

He chuckled. "Something like that."

"How come you're not married already and starting that family?"

He ran his fingers through his short-cropped, sandy-brown hair. "Haven't had time."

"No?"

"I was born and raised in Moscow, Idaho, and I'm the only boy in a family of three kids. I enrolled in Bible college shortly after I graduated high school, but I never finished."

"I take it you're a Christian, too?"

He nodded. "My conversion came when I was a teenager."

"How come you never finished Bible college?" she questioned.

"I decided on a tour of duty with the United States Air Force instead." A muscle jerked in his cheek, and he frowned slightly. "I had a relationship with a woman go sour on me. After praying about it, I figured the best way to get over her was to enlist and get as far away from the state of Idaho as I could."

In the few weeks she'd known Evan, this was the first time Lorna had seen him look so serious, and it took her completely by surprise. She was trying to decide how to comment, when the waitress showed up with their pizza. Lorna was almost relieved at the interruption. At least now she could concentrate on filling her stomach and not her mind.

After a brief prayer, Evan began attacking his pizza with a vengeance. It made Lorna wonder when his last good meal had been. By the time she'd finished two pieces, Evan had polished off four slices and was working on another one. He glanced at Lorna's plate. "Aren't you hungry?"

"The pizza is great. I'm enjoying every bite," she said.

He swiped the napkin across his face and stared at Lorna. It made her squirm.

"Why are you looking at me that way?"

"What way?"

"Like I've got something on my face."

He chuckled. "Your face is spotless. I was thinking how much I enjoy your company and wondering if we might have a future together."

Lorna nearly choked on the piece of pizza she'd just put in her mouth. "Well, I — uh — don't think we're very well suited, and isn't it a little soon to be talking about a future together?"

"I'm not ready to propose marriage, if that's what you're thinking." His eyes narrowed. "And please don't tell me you're hung up about our age difference." Evan looked at Lorna so intently she could feel her toes curl inside her tennis shoes.

"That doesn't bother me so much. We're only talking about four years."

"Right." Evan raised his eyebrows. "You couldn't be afraid of men, or you wouldn't have been married before."

"I am not afraid of men! Why do you do that, anyway?"

"Do what?"

"Try to goad me into an argument."

He chuckled behind another slice of pizza. "Is that what you think I'm doing?"

"Isn't it?"

He dropped the pizza to his plate, reached across the table, and took hold of her hand.

She shivered involuntarily and averted her gaze to the table. "I wish you wouldn't do that either."

"Do what? This?" He made little circles on her hand with his index finger.

She felt warmth travel up her neck and spread quickly to her cheeks. "The way you look at me, I almost feel —"

"Like you're a beautiful, desirable woman?" He leaned farther across the table. "You are, you know. And I don't care about you being four years older than me. In fact, I think dating an older woman might have some advantages."

She pulled her hand away. "And what would those be?"

He crossed his arms and leaned back in his seat. "Let's see now. . . . You'd be more apt to see things from a mature point of view."

"And?"

"Just a minute. I'm thinking." Evan tapped the edge of his plate with his thumb. "Since you're older, you're most likely wiser."

She clicked her tongue. "Sorry I asked."

"Would you be willing to start dating me?" he asked with a hopeful expression.

She shook her head. "I'm flattered you would ask, but I don't think it's a good idea."

"Why not?"

Something indefinable passed between them, but Lorna pushed it aside. "I have my heart set on finishing college, and nothing is going to stop me this time."

He gave her a quizzical look. "This time?"

Lorna ended up telling him the story of how she'd sacrificed her own career and college degree to put her husband through school. She ended it by saying, "So, you see, for the first time in a long while, I'm finally getting what I want."

"That's it? End of story?"

She nodded. "It will be when I graduate and get a job teaching music at an elementary school."

"Why not teach at a junior or senior high?"

"I like children — especially those young enough to be molded and refined." She wrinkled her nose. "The older a child is, the harder to get through to his creativity."

"Does that mean I won't be able to get through to your creative side?" he asked with a lopsided grin.

"Could be." She folded her napkin into a neat little square and lifted her chin. "I really need to get home. I've got a lot of homework to do, and I've wasted most of the day."

Evan's sudden scowl told her she'd obviously hurt his feelings. "I didn't mean *wasted.* It's just that —"

He held up his hand. "No explanations are necessary." He stood, pulled a few coins from his back pocket, and dropped them on the table. "I hope that's enough for a tip, 'cause it's all the change I have."

She fumbled in her jacket pocket. "Maybe I have some ones I could add."

"Please don't bother. This will be enough, and I sure don't expect you to pay for the tip."

"I don't mind helping out," she insisted.

"Thanks anyway, but I'll take care of it." With that, Evan turned and headed for the cash register.

Lorna stood there with her ears burning and her heart pounding so hard she could hear it echoing in her ears. The day had started off so well. What had gone wrong, and how had it happened?

Evan was already up front paying for the pizza, so Lorna dug into her pocket and pulled out a dollar bill, which she quickly dropped to the table. Maybe she'd made a mistake thinking she and Evan could be friends. He obviously wanted more, but she knew it was impossible. In fact, he was impossible. Impossible and poor.

Evan said good-bye to Lorna outside in the parking lot. He was almost glad they had separate cars and he wouldn't have to drive her home. He didn't understand how a day that had started out fun and carefree could have ended on such a sour note. From all indications, he'd thought Lorna was enjoying their time together, but when she said she'd wasted most of the day, he felt deflated, even though he hadn't admitted it to her. That, plus the fact that she seemed overly concerned about his not having enough tip money, had thrown cold water on their time together.

What had turned things around? Had it been the discussion about their age difference? Children? Or maybe it was the money thing. Lorna might think he'd been too cheap to leave a decent tip. That could be why she'd climbed into her little red car with barely a wave and said nothing about hoping to see him again. Of course, he hadn't made the first move on that account either.

"I thought she might be the one, Lord," Evan mumbled as he opened the door to his Jeep. Remembering the look on Lorna's face when she'd eaten the treat he'd given her earlier that day, he added, "Maybe I should have followed the recipe closer and added some chocolate chips to the top of those brownies."

# CHAPTER 7

The following Monday morning in Anatomy, Evan acted as though nothing were wrong. In fact, he surprised Lorna by presenting her with a wedge of apple pie he said he'd made the night before.

"It's a little mushy, and the crust's kind of tough," he admitted, "but I sampled a slice at breakfast, and it seemed sweet enough, at least."

Lorna smiled politely and took the plastic container with the pie in it. It was nice of Evan to think of her, but if he thought the dessert would give him an edge, he was mistaken. Lorna was fighting her attraction to Evan, and to lead him on would sooner or later cause one or both of them to get hurt.

*Probably me,* she thought. *I'm usually the one who makes all the sacrifices, then loses in the end.* What good had come out of her putting Ron through college and med school? He'd been killed in a senseless accident, leaving Lorna with a broken heart, a mound of bills, and no career for herself. It was going to be different from now on though. She finally had her life back on track.

"You look kind of down in the mouth this morning," Evan said, nudging her arm gently with his hand. "Everything okay?"

She shrugged. "I'm just tired. I

stayed up late last night trying to get all my homework done."

He pursed his lips. "Guess that's my fault. If you hadn't wasted your Saturday bike riding and having pizza with me, you'd have had lots more time to work on your assignments."

So Evan had been hurt by her comment about wasted time on Saturday. Lorna could see by the look in the man's eyes that his pride was wounded. She felt a sense of guilt sweep over her like a cascading waterfall. She hadn't meant to hurt him. As a Christian, Lorna tried not to offend anyone, although she probably had fallen short many times since Ron's death.

"Evan," she began sincerely, "I apologize for my offhanded remark the other day. I had a good time with you, and my day wasn't wasted."

He grinned at her. "Really?"

She nodded.

"Would you be willing to go out with me again — as friends?"

Lorna chewed on her lower lip as she contemplated his offer. "Well, maybe," she finally conceded.

"That's great! How about this Saturday night, if you've got the evening off from working at Farmen's."

"I only work on weeknights," she said.

"Good, then we can go bowling, out to dinner, to the movies . . . or all three."

She chuckled softly. "I think one of those would be sufficient, don't you?"

"Yeah, I suppose so. Which one's your choice?"

"Why don't you surprise me on

Saturday night?"

"Okay, I will." Evan snapped his fingers. "Say, I'll need your address so I can pick you up."

Lorna felt as though a glass of cold water had been dashed in her face. There was no way she could allow Evan to come by her in-laws' and pick her up for what she was sure they would assume was a date. She couldn't hurt Ann and Ed that way. It wouldn't be fair to Ron's memory. Maybe she should have told Evan she was busy on Saturday night. Maybe . . .

"You gonna give me your address or not?"

Lorna blinked. "Uh — how about we meet somewhere, like we did last Saturday?"

His forehead wrinkled. "Are you

ashamed for your folks to meet me?"

"I live with my in-laws, remember?"

"So?"

"They might not understand about my going out with you," she explained. "They're still not over the loss of their son."

Evan stared at her for several seconds but finally shrugged his shoulders. "Okay. If that's how you want it, we can meet at Ivar's along the waterfront. I've been wanting to try out their famous fish and chips ever since I came to Seattle."

Lorna licked her lips. "That does sound good."

Evan opened his mouth to say something more, but their professor walked into the room. "We'll talk later," he whispered.

She nodded in response.

Lorna entered the choir room a few minutes early, hoping to get her music organized before class began. She noticed Evan standing by the bulletin board across the room. She hated to admit it, but he was fun to be around. Could he be growing on her?

When she took a seat at the piano and peeked over the stack of music, she saw Vanessa Brown step up beside Evan. "Are the names posted for the choir solos yet?" the vivacious redhead asked. "I sure hope I got the female lead." She looked up at Evan and batted her lashes. "Maybe you'll get the male lead, and then we can practice together. Our voices would blend beautifully, don't you think?"

*Oh please,* Lorna groaned inwardly. The omelet she'd eaten for breakfast that morning had suddenly turned into a lump in the pit of her stomach. She didn't like the sly little grin Evan was wearing, either. He was up to something, and it probably meant someone was in for a double dose of his teasing.

Evan stepped in front of Vanessa, blocking her view of the board. She let out a grunt and tugged on his shirtsleeve. "I can't see. What's it say?"

Evan held his position, mumbling something Lorna couldn't quite understand.

"Well?" Vanessa shouted. "Are you going to tell me what it says or not?"

He scratched the back of his head. "Hmm . . ."

"What is it? Let me see!"

Evan glanced over at Lorna, but she quickly averted her gaze, pretending to be absorbed in her music.

When she lifted her head, Lorna saw Vanessa slide under Evan's arm, until she was facing the bulletin board. She studied it for several seconds, but then her hands dropped to her hips and she whirled around. "That just figures!" She marched across the room and stopped in front of the piano, shooting Lorna a look that could have stopped traffic on the busy Seattle freeway. "I hope you're satisfied!"

Lorna was bewildered. "What are you talking about?"

"Professor Burrows chose *you* for the female solo!" Vanessa scowled at Lorna. "Just because you're older than the rest of us and play the piano fairly well shouldn't mean you get special privileges."

Lorna creased her forehead so hard she felt wrinkles form. "Why would you say such a thing?"

"The professor doesn't think you can do any wrong. She's always telling the class how mature you are and how you're the only one who ever follows directions."

Lorna opened her mouth to offer some kind of rebuttal, but before she got a word out, Evan's deep voice cut her off. "Now wait a minute, Vanessa. Lorna got the lead part for only one reason."

Vanessa turned to face Evan, who stood at her side in front of the piano. "And that would be?"

"This talented woman can not only

play the piano, but she can sing. Beautifully, I might add." He cast Lorna a sidelong glance, and she felt the heat of a blush warm her cheeks.

Vanessa's dark eyes narrowed. "Are you saying *I* can't sing?"

"I don't think that's what he meant," Lorna interjected.

Vanessa slapped her hand on the piano keys with such force that Lorna worried the Baldwin might never be the same. "Let the man speak for himself!" She whirled around to face Evan. "Or does the cute little blond have you so wrapped around her finger that you can't even think straight? It's obvious you're smitten with her."

Evan opened his mouth as if he was going to say something, but Vanessa cut him off. "Don't try to deny it,

Evan Bailey! I've seen the way you and Lorna look at each other." She sniffed deeply. "Is she trying to rob from the cradle, or are you looking for a mother figure?"

Evan's face had turned crimson. "I think this discussion is over," he said firmly.

"That's right — let's drop it," Lorna agreed.

Vanessa glared at Evan. "Be a good boy now, and do what Mama Lorna says."

He drew in a deep breath. "I'm warning you, Vanessa . . ."

"What are you going to do? Tell the teacher on me?" she taunted.

Lorna cleared her throat a couple of times, and both Evan and Vanessa turned to look at her. "We're all adults here, and if getting the lead part means so much to you, I'll speak to the professor about it, Vanessa."

"I'll fight my own battles, thank you very much!" Vanessa squared her shoulders. "Unlike some people in this class, I don't need a mother to fix my boo-boos." She turned on her heels and marched out of the room.

Evan let out a low whistle. "What was that all about?"

Lorna shook her head slowly. "You don't know?"

He shrugged. "Not really. She said she wanted the solo part, you offered to give it to her, and she's still mad. Makes no sense to me." He snickered. "But then, I never was much good at understanding women. Even if I did grow up with two sisters."

Lorna pinched the bridge of her nose. How could the man be so blind? "Vanessa is jealous."

"I know. She wants your part," Evan said, dropping to the bench beside Lorna. "She can't stand the fact that someone has a better singing voice than she does."

"I think the real reason Vanessa's jealous is because she thinks you like me, and she's attracted to you."

Evan looked at Lorna as though she'd lost her mind. "I've done nothing to make Vanessa think she and I might —"

"That doesn't matter. You make people laugh, and your manner is often flirtatious."

Evan rubbed his chin and frowned. "What can I say? I'm a friendly guy, but that doesn't mean I'm after every woman I meet."

Lorna reached for a piece of music. "Tell that to Vanessa Brown."

# CHAPTER 8

Evan moved away from the piano, wishing there were something he could say or do to make Lorna feel more comfortable about the part she'd gotten. The scene with Vanessa had been unreal, but the fact that Lorna was willing to give up the solo part she'd been offered was one more proof that she lived her Christianity and would make a good wife for some lucky man. It just probably wasn't him.

He took a seat in the chair he'd been assigned and studied Lorna.

She was thumbing through a stack of music, her forehead wrinkled and her face looking pinched. Was she still thinking about the encounter with Vanessa, frustrated with Evan, or merely trying to concentrate on getting ready for their first choir number?

Not only was Lorna a beautiful, talented musician, but she had a sensitivity that drew Evan to her like a powerful magnet. Anyone willing to give up a favored part and not get riled when Vanessa attacked her with a vengeance made a hit with Evan. Lorna had done the Christian thing, even if Vanessa hadn't. Now if he could only convince her to give their relationship a chance. Maybe their

Saturday night date would turn the tide.

Lorna had just slipped on her Farmen's apron when Chris came up behind her. "How was school today?"

"Don't ask."

"That bad, huh?"

"Afraid so."

"You've been back in college for a couple of weeks. I thought you'd be getting used to the routine by now."

Lorna grabbed an order pad from the back of the counter and stuffed it in her apron pocket. "The routine's not the problem."

Chris's forehead wrinkled. "What is, then?"

Lorna rubbed the back of her neck, trying to get the kinks out. "Never mind. It's probably not worth mentioning."

"It doesn't have anything to do with Evan Bailey, does it?"

"No! Yes. Well, partially."

Chris glanced at the clock on the wall above the serving counter. "We've still got a few minutes until our shift starts. Let's go to the ladies' room, and you can tell me about it."

Lorna shook her head. "What's the point? Talking won't change anything."

Chris grabbed her arm and gave it a gentle tug. "Come on, friend. I know you'll feel better once you've opened up and told me what's bothering you."

"Oh, all right," Lorna mumbled. "Let's hurry though. I don't want to get docked any pay for starting late."

Lorna was glad to discover an

empty ladies' room when she and Chris arrived a few moments later. Chris dropped onto the small leather couch and motioned Lorna to do the same. "Okay, spill it!"

Lorna curled up in one corner of the couch and let the whole story out, beginning with her entering the choir room that morning and ending with Vanessa's juvenile tantrum and Evan's response to it all.

Chris folded her hands across her stomach and laughed. It wasn't some weak, polite little giggle, like Lorna offered her customers. It was a genuine, full-blown belly laugh.

Lorna didn't see what was so funny. In fact, retelling the story had only upset her further. "This is no laughing matter, Chris. It's serious business."

Her friend blinked a couple of times and then burst into another round of laughter.

Lorna started to get up. "Okay, fine! I shouldn't have said anything to you — that's obvious."

Chris reached over and grabbed hold of Lorna's arm. "No, stay, please." She wiped her eyes with the back of her hand. "I hope you know I wasn't laughing at you."

"Who?"

"The whole scenario." Chris clicked her tongue. "I just don't get you, Lorna."

"What do you mean?"

"Evan Bailey is one cute guy, right?"

Lorna nodded and flopped back onto the couch.

"From what you've told me, I'd say the man has high moral standards and is lots of fun to be with."

"Yes."

Chris leaned toward Lorna. "If you don't wake up and hear the music, you might lose the terrific guy to this Vanessa person. If I'd been you today, I don't think I could have been so nice about things." She grimaced. "Offering to give up the part — now that's Christianity in action!"

Lorna crossed her legs and swung her foot back and forth, thinking the whole while how tempted she had been to give that feisty redhead a swift kick this afternoon. She'd said what she felt was right at the time, but it hadn't been easy.

"From all you've told me, I'd say it's pretty obvious the woman has her sights set on Evan Bailey." Chris shook her finger at Lorna. "You need to put this whole age thing out of your mind and give the guy a chance."

Lorna cringed. "That's not really the problem. I think Evan is as poor as a church mouse."

"What gives you that idea?"

Lorna quickly related the story of her and Evan's bicycle ride and how when they'd had pizza, he didn't have enough money to leave a decent tip.

Chris groaned. "Don't you think you're jumping to conclusions? Maybe the guy just didn't have much cash on him that day." She squinted her eyes. "And even if he is dirt poor, does it really matter so much?"

"It does to me. I don't want to get involved with another man who will expect me to give up my career and put him through college."

■ ■ ■ ■

Evan was excited about his date with Lorna tonight. He'd been looking forward to it all week and had even tried his hand at making another on-line sweet treat, which he planned to give Lorna after dinner this evening. It was called Lemon Supreme and consisted of cream cheese mixed with lemon juice, sugar, eggs, and vanilla. Graham cracker crumbs were used for the crust, and confectioner's sugar was sprinkled over the top. He hadn't had time to sample it, but Evan was sure Lorna would like it.

At six o'clock sharp, Evan stood in front of Ivar's Restaurant along the Seattle waterfront. He was pleased when he saw Lorna cross the street and head in his direction. He'd been worried she might stand him up.

"Am I late?" she panted. "I had a hard time finding a place to park."

"You're right on time," he assured her. "I got here a few minutes ago and put my name on the waiting list at the restaurant."

"How long did they say we might have to wait for a table?"

"Not more than a half hour or so," he said.

"Guess we could go inside and wait in the lobby."

Evan nodded. "Or we could stay out here awhile and enjoy the night air." He drew in a deep breath. "Ah, sure does smell fresh down by the water, doesn't it?"

She wrinkled her nose. "Guess that all depends on what you call fresh."

"Salt sea air and fish a-frying . . .

now that's what I call fresh," he countered with a wide smile.

She poked him playfully on the arm. "You would say something like that."

He chuckled. "Ah, you know me so well."

"No, actually, I don't," she said with a slight frown.

"Then we need to remedy that." Evan gazed deeply into her eyes. "I'd sure like to know you better, 'cause what I've seen so far I really like."

Lorna gulped. Things were moving too fast, and she seemed powerless to stop them. What had happened to her resolve not to get involved with another man, or even to date? She had to put a stop to this before it escalated into more than friendship.

Before she had a chance to open

her mouth, Evan took hold of her hand and led her to a bench along the side of the building. It faced the water, where several docks were located. "Let's sit awhile and watch the boats come and go," he suggested.

"What about our dinner reservations?"

"They said they'd call my name over the loudspeaker when our table's ready. Fortunately, there's a speaker outside, too." Evan sat down, and Lorna did the same.

The ferry coming from Bremerton docked, and Lorna watched the people disembark. She hadn't been to Bremerton in a long time. She hardly went anywhere but work, school, church, and shopping once in a while. What had happened to the carefree days of vacations, fun evenings out, and days off? *Guess I gave those things up when I began working so Ron could go to school.* Working two jobs left little time for fun or recreation, and now that Lorna was in school and still employed at one job, things weren't much better. *I do have the weekends free,* her conscience reminded. *Maybe I deserve to have a little fun now and then.*

"You look like you're a hundred miles away," Evan said, breaking into her thoughts.

She turned her head and looked at him. "I was watching the ferry."

He lifted her chin with his hand. "And I've been watching you."

Before Lorna could respond, he tipped his head and brushed a gentle kiss against her lips. As the kiss deepened, she instinctively wrapped her arms around his neck.

"Bailey, party of two . . . your table is ready!"

Lorna jerked away from Evan at the sound of his name being called over the loudspeaker. "We–we'd better get in there," she said breathlessly.

"Right." Evan stood up, pulling Lorna gently to her feet.

She went silently by his side into the restaurant, berating herself for allowing that kiss. *I'll be on my guard the rest of the evening. No more dreamy looks and no more kisses!*

# CHAPTER 9

Farmen's Restaurant was more
crowded than usual on Monday
night, and Lorna's boss had just
informed her that they were short-
handed. With God's help, she would
get through her shift, although she
was already tired. It had been a busy
weekend, and she'd had to cram in
time for homework.

Lorna thought about her date with
Evan on Saturday, which hadn't
ended until eleven o'clock because
they'd taken a ride on one of the
sightseeing boats after dinner. She'd

thoroughly enjoyed the moonlight cruise around Puget Sound, and when Evan walked Lorna to her car, he'd presented her with another of his desserts. This one was called Lemon Supreme, and she had tried it after she got home that night.

Lorna puckered her lips as she remembered the sour taste caused by either too much lemon juice or not enough sugar. *I doubt Evan will ever be a master baker,* she mused.

She glanced at her reflection in the mirror over the serving counter, checking her uniform and hair one last time as she contemplated the way Evan had looked at her before they'd said good night. He'd wanted to kiss her again; she could tell by his look of longing. She had prevented it from happening by jumping quickly into her car and shutting the door.

"I only want to be his friend," Lorna muttered under her breath as she strolled into the dining room.

She got right to work and took the order of an elderly couple. Then she moved across the aisle to where another couple sat with their heads bent over the menus.

The woman was the first to look up, and Lorna's mouth dropped open.

"Fancy meeting you here," Vanessa Brown drawled.

Before Lorna could respond, Vanessa's companion looked up and announced, "Lorna works here."

Lorna's hand began to tremble, and she dropped the order pad. Evan Bailey was looking at her as though nothing was wrong. Maybe his having dinner with Vanessa was a normal occurrence. Maybe this wasn't their first date.

Forcing her thoughts to remain on the business at hand, Lorna bent down to retrieve the pad. When she stood up again, Vanessa was leaning across the table, fussing with Evan's shirt collar.

Lorna cleared her throat, and Vanessa glanced over at her. "What's good to eat in this place?"

"Tonight's special is meat loaf." Lorna kept her focus on the order pad.

"Meat loaf sounds good to me," Evan said.

"You're such a simple, easy-to-please kind of guy," Vanessa fairly purred.

Lorna swallowed back the urge to scream. She probably shouldn't be having these unwarranted feelings of jealousy, for she had no claim on Evan. He'd obviously lied to her the other day, when he denied any interest in Vanessa. A guy didn't take a girl out to dinner if he didn't care something about her. *He took me to dinner on Saturday. Does that mean he cares about both me and Vanessa? Or could Evan Bailey be toying with our emotions?*

Lorna turned to face Vanessa, feeling as though the air between them was charged with electricity. "What would you like to order?"

"I'm careful about what I eat, so I think I'll have a chicken salad with low-cal ranch dressing." Vanessa looked over at her dinner partner and batted her eyelashes. "Men like their women to be fit and trim, right,

Evan?"

He shrugged his shoulders. "I can't speak for other men, but to my way of thinking, it's what's in a woman's heart that really matters. Outward appearances can sometimes be deceiving."

He cast Lorna a grin, and she tapped her pencil against the order pad impatiently. "Will there be anything else?"

Evan opened his mouth. "Yes, actually —"

"Why don't you bring us a couple of sugar-free mocha-flavored coffees?" Vanessa interrupted. She gave Evan a syrupy smile. "I hope you like that flavor."

"Well, I —"

"Two mochas, a meat loaf special, and one chicken salad, coming right up!" Lorna turned on her heels and hurried away.

Evan watched Lorna's retreating form. Her shoulders were hunched, and her head was down. Obviously she wasn't at her best. He could tell she'd been trying to be polite when she took their orders, but from her tone of voice and those wrinkles he'd noticed on her forehead, he was certain she was irritated about something.

*Probably wondering what I'm doing here with Vanessa. Wish she had stuck around longer so I could have explained. Maybe I should have gone after her.*

"Evan, are you listening to me?"

Evan turned his head. "What were you saying, Vanessa?"

"I'm glad I ran into you tonight. I wanted to ask your opinion on something."

"What's that?"

Vanessa leaned her elbows on the table and intertwined her fingers. "All day I've been thinking about that solo part I should have had."

"You're coming to grips with it, I hope."

She frowned. "Actually, I've been wondering whether I should have taken Lorna up on her offer to give the part to me. What do you think, Evan? Should I ask her about it when she returns with our orders?"

Evan grunted. "I can't believe you'd really expect her to give you that solo. Professor Burrows obviously feels Lorna's the best one for the part, or she wouldn't have assigned it to her."

Vanessa wrinkled her nose. "And I can't believe the way you always stick up for that little blond. She's too old and too prim and proper for you, Evan. Why don't you wake up?"

Evan reached for his glass of water and took a big gulp, hoping to regain his composure before he spoke again. When he set the glass down, he leaned forward and looked Vanessa right in the eye. "I'm not hung up on age differences, and as far as Lorna being prim and proper, you don't know what you're talking about."

Vanessa blinked and pulled back like she'd been stung by a bee. "You don't have to be so mean, Evan. I was only trying to make you see how much better —"

She was interrupted when Lorna appeared at the table with their orders. Evan was glad he could concentrate on eating his meat loaf instead of trying to change Vanessa's mind about a woman she barely knew.

As Lorna placed Evan's plate in front of him, she was greeted with another one of his phony smiles. They had to be phony. No man in his right mind would be out with one woman and flirting with another. For that matter, most men didn't bring their date to the workplace of the woman he'd dated only two nights before. *Dated and kissed,* she fumed.

Lorna excused herself to get their beverages, and a short time later she returned with two mugs of mocha-flavored coffee. She looked at Evan sitting across from Vanessa, and an unexpected yearning stirred within her soul. Why couldn't she be the one he was having dinner with tonight? All this time Lorna had been telling herself that she and Evan could only be friends, so it didn't make sense to feel jealousy over seeing him with Vanessa Brown.

*Maybe I don't know my own heart. Maybe . . .*

"This isn't low-cal dressing. I asked for low-cal, remember?"

Vanessa's sharp words pulled Lorna's disconcerting thoughts aside. "I think it is," she replied. "I turned in an order for low-cal dressing, and I'm sure —"

"I just tasted it. It's not low-cal!"

Lorna drew in a deep breath and offered up a quick prayer for patience. "I'll go check with the cook who filled your order."

She started to turn, but Vanessa shouted, "I want another salad! This one is drenched in fattening ranch dressing, and it's ruined."

Lorna was so aggravated her ears were ringing, yet she knew in order to keep her job at Farmen's she would need to be polite to all customers — even someone as demanding as Vanessa. "I'll be back with another salad."

As she was turning in the order for the salad, Lorna met up with her friend Chris.

"You don't look like the picture of happiness tonight," Chris noted. "What's the problem — too many customers?"

Lorna gritted her teeth. "Just two too many."

"What's that supposed to mean?"

Lorna explained about Evan and Vanessa being on a date and how Vanessa was demanding a new salad.

Chris squinted her eyes. "I thought you and Evan went to Ivar's on Saturday."

"We did."

"Then what's up with him bringing another woman here on a date?"

Lorna leaned against the edge of the serving counter and groaned. "He's two-faced. What can I say?"

"Want me to finish up with that table for you?"

Lorna sighed with relief. "Would you? I don't think I can face Evan and his date again tonight."

Chris patted Lorna's arm. "Sure. What are friends for?"

Lorna peered into the darkening sky,

watching out the window as Evan and Vanessa left the restaurant. She thought it was strange when she saw them each get into their own cars, but she shrugged it off, remembering that she and Evan had taken separate vehicles on Saturday night. Maybe Evan didn't have time to pick Vanessa up for their date. Maybe she'd been out running errands. It didn't matter. Lorna's shift would be over in a few hours, and then she could go home, indulge in a long, hot bath, and crash on the couch in front of the fireplace. Maybe a cup of hot chocolate and some of Ann's famous oatmeal cookies would help soothe her frazzled nerves. Some pleasant music and a good inspirational novel to read could have her feeling better in no time.

Lorna moved away from the window and sought out her next customer. She had a job to do, and she wouldn't waste another minute thinking about Evan Bailey. If he desired someone as self-serving as Vanessa Brown, he could have her.

Determined to come up with a way to win Lorna's heart, Evan had decided to try another recipe from his online cooking class. This one was called Bodacious Banana Bread, and it looked fairly simple to make. Between the loaf of bread and the explanation he planned to give Lorna tomorrow at school, Evan hoped he could let her know how much he cared.

Whistling to the tune of "Jesus Loves Me," Evan set out the ingredients he needed: butter, honey, eggs, flour, salt, soda, baking powder, and two ripe bananas. In short order he had everything mixed. He poured the batter into a glass baking dish and pulled it off the counter. Suddenly his hand bumped a bowl of freshly washed blueberries he planned to have with a dish of vanilla ice cream later on. The bowl toppled over, and half the blueberries tumbled into the bread pan, on top of the banana mixture.

"Oh no," Evan moaned. "Now I've done it." He tried to pick the blueberries out, but too many had already sunk to the bottom of the pan.

"Guess I could bake it as is and hope for the best." Evan grabbed a wooden spoon and gave the dough a couple of stirs to ensure that the berries were evenly distributed. He figured it couldn't turn out any worse than the other desserts he'd foiled since he first began the cooking class. That Lemon Supreme he'd been dumb enough to give Lorna without first tasting had been one of the worst. He'd sampled a piece after their date on Saturday night and realized he'd messed up the recipe somehow, because it wasn't sweet enough.

Two hours later the bread was done and had cooled sufficiently. Evan decided to try a slice, determined not to give any to Lorna if it tasted funny.

To Evan's delight, the bread was wonderful. The blueberries had added a nice texture to the sweet dessert, and it was cooked to perfection. "I think I'll call this my Blueberry

Surprise," he said with a chuckle. "Sure hope it impresses Lorna, because I'm not certain I have any words that will."

# CHAPTER 10

Going back to school the following day — knowing she would have to face both Evan and Vanessa — was difficult for Lorna. She didn't know why it should be so hard. Evan had made no commitment to her, nor she to him.

When she arrived at school, Lorna was surprised to see Evan standing in the hall just outside their anatomy class. He spotted her, waved, and held up a paper sack. "I have something for you, and we need to talk." His voice sounded almost pleading, and that in itself Lorna found unsettling.

"There's nothing to talk about." Lorna started to walk away, hoping to avoid any confrontations and knowing if they did talk, her true feelings might give her away.

Evan reached out and grabbed hold of her arm. When she turned to face him, he lifted his free hand and wrapped a tendril of her hair around his finger. He leaned slightly forward — so close she could feel his breath on her upturned face. If she didn't do something quickly, she was sure she was about to be kissed.

Evan moved his finger from her hair to her face, skimming down her cheek, then along her chin.

Lorna shivered with a mixture of anticipation and dread, knowing she should pull away. Just as Evan's lips sought hers, the floor began to move and the walls swayed back and forth in a surreal manner. Lorna had heard of bells going off and being so much in love that it hurt, but if this weird sensation had anything to do with the way she felt about Evan, she didn't want any part of loving the man.

Evan grasped Lorna's shoulders as the floor tilted, and she almost lost her balance. Knowing she needed his support in order to stay on her feet, Lorna leaned into him, gripping both of his arms. "What's happening?" she rasped.

"I believe we're in the middle of a bad earthquake." Evan's face seemed etched with concern. It was a stark contrast from his usual smiling expression.

Lorna's eyes widened with dread. She looked down and thought she was going to be sick. The floor was moving rhythmically up and down. It reminded her of a ship caught in a storm, about to be capsized with the crest of each angry wave.

"This is a bad one!" Evan exclaimed. "We need to get under a table or something."

She looked around helplessly; there were no tables in the hall and none in the anatomy class either. The room only had opera-style seats. "Where?"

Evan pulled her closer. "A doorway! We should stand under a doorway."

The door to their classroom was only a few feet away, but it took great effort for them to maneuver themselves into position. Lorna's heart was thumping so hard she was sure

Evan could hear each radical beat. She'd been in a few earthquakes during her lifetime, but none so violent as this one.

A candy machine in the hallway vibrated, pictures on the wall flew in every direction, and a terrible, cracking sound rent the air as the windows rattled and broke. A loud crash, followed by a shrill scream, sent shivers up Lorna's spine. There was no one else in the hallway, which was unusual, considering the fact that classes were scheduled to begin soon. Where was everybody, and when would this nightmare end?

Another ear-piercing sound! Was that a baby's cry? No, it couldn't be. This was Bay View Christian College, not a daycare center.

"I think the scream came from over

there," Evan said, pointing across the hall. He glanced down at Lorna. "Did that sound like a baby's cry to you?"

She nodded and swallowed against the lump lodged in her throat.

"Stay here. I'll be right back." Evan handed Lorna the paper sack he'd been holding.

"No, don't leave me!" She clutched the front of his shirt as panic swept through her in a wave so cold and suffocating, she thought she might faint.

"I think you'll be okay if you wait right here," he assured her. "Pray, Lorna. Pray."

The walls and floor were still moving, though a bit slower now. Lorna watched helplessly as Evan half crawled, half slid on his stomach across the hall. When he disappeared behind the door, she sent up a prayer. "Dear God, please keep him safe."

At that moment, the truth slammed into Lorna with a force stronger than any earthquake. Although she hadn't known Evan very long, she was falling in love with him. In the few short weeks since they'd met, he had brought joy and laughter into her life. He'd made her feel beautiful and special, something she hadn't felt since Ron's untimely death. They had a common bond. Both were Christians and interested in music, and each had a desire to work with children.

*Children.* The word stuck in Lorna's brain. She had always wanted a child. When she married Ron, Lorna was sure they would start a family as soon as he finished med school. That never happened because her husband had been snatched away as quickly as fog settles over Puget Sound.

She leaned heavily against the door frame and let this new revelation sink in. Was going back to school and getting her degree really Lorna's heart's desire? Or was being married to someone she loved and starting a family what she truly wanted? *It doesn't matter. I can't have a relationship with Evan because he doesn't love me. He's been seeing Vanessa.*

"Lorna! Can you come over here?" Evan's urgent plea broke into her thoughts, and she reeled at the sound of his resonating voice.

The earthquake was over now, but Lorna knew from past experience that a series of smaller tremors would no doubt follow. She made her way carefully across the hall and into the room she'd seen Evan enter only moments ago.

She stopped short inside the door. In the middle of the room lay a young woman. A bookcase had fallen across her legs, pinning her to the floor. Lorna gasped as she realized the woman was holding a crying baby in her arms. The sight brought tears to Lorna's eyes. Covering her mouth to stifle a sob, she raced to Evan's side and dropped down beside him. She noticed beads of perspiration glistening on his upper lip. "Is she hurt badly? What about the baby?" Tears rolled down Lorna's cheeks as she thought about the possibility of a child losing its mother, or the other way around. *Please, God, let them be all right.*

"The woman's legs could be broken, so it wouldn't be good to try to move her. The baby appears to be okay." He pointed to the sobbing infant. "Could you pick her up, then go down the hall and find a phone? We need to call 911 right away."

Lorna nodded numbly. As soon as she lifted the child into her arms, the baby's crying abated. She stood and started for the door. Looking back over her shoulder, she whispered, "I love you, Evan, even if you do care for Vanessa Brown."

The next few hours went by in a blur. A trip to the hospital in Evan's car, following the ambulance that transported the injured woman . . . Talking with the paramedics who'd found some identification on the baby's mother. Calling the woman's husband on the phone. Pacing the floor of the hospital waiting room. Trying to comfort a fussy child. Waiting patiently until the father arrived. Praying until no more words would come. Lorna did all these things with Evan by her side. They said little to each other as they waited to hear of the mother's condition. Words seemed unnecessary as Lorna acknowledged a shared sense of oneness with Evan, found only in a crisis situation.

The woman, who'd been identified as Sherry Holmes, had been at the college that morning looking for her husband, an English professor. He'd left for work without his briefcase, and she'd come to deliver the papers he needed. Professor Holmes wasn't in his class when she arrived. He'd been to an early morning meeting in another building, as had most of the other teachers. Why there weren't any other students in the hallway, Lorna still did not understand. She thought it must have been divine intervention, since so much structural damage had been done to that particular building. Who knew how many more injuries might have occurred had there been numerous students milling about?

Lorna felt a sense of loss as she handed the baby over to her father a short time later. She was relieved to hear that the child's mother was in stable condition, despite a broken leg and several bad bruises.

"You look done in," Evan said, taking Lorna's hand and leading her to a chair. He pointed to the paper sack lying on the table in the waiting room, where Lorna had placed it when they first arrived. "You never did open your present."

She nodded and offered him a weak smile. "Guess I've been too busy with other things." She pulled it open and peeked inside. A sweet banana aroma overtook her senses, and she sniffed deeply. "I'm guessing it's a loaf of banana bread."

Evan smiled. "It started out to be, but in the end, it turned out to be a kind of blueberry surprise."

She tipped her head and squinted her eyes. "What?"

Evan chuckled. "It's a long story." He motioned to the sack. "Try a hunk. I think you'll be pleasantly surprised."

Lorna opened the bag and withdrew a piece of the bread. She took a tentative bite, remembering the other treats he'd given her that hadn't turned out so well. To her surprise, the blueberry-banana bread was actually good. It was wonderful, in fact. She grinned at him. "This is great. You should patent the recipe."

He smiled and reached for her hand. "I don't know what surprises me the most . . . the accidental making of a great-tasting bread or your willingness to be here with me now."

"It's been a pretty rough morning, and I'm thankful the baby and her mother are going to be okay," she said, making no reference to her willingness to be with Evan.

"The look of gratitude on Professor

Holmes's face will stay with me a long time." Evan gazed deeply into Lorna's eyes. "Nothing is as precious as the life God gives each of us, and I don't want to waste a single moment of the time I have left on this earth." He stroked the side of her face tenderly. "You're the most precious gift He's ever offered me."

Lorna blinked back sudden tears. "Me? But I thought you and Vanessa —"

Evan shook his head and leaned over to kiss her. When he pulled away, he smiled. Not his usual silly grin, but an honest "I love you" kind of smile. "I came to the restaurant last night to talk to you," he said. "I was going to plead my case and beg you to give our relationship a try."

"But Vanessa —"

"She was not my date."

"She wasn't?"

He shook his head.

"You were both at the same table, and I thought —"

"I know what you thought." He wrapped his arms around Lorna and held her tightly. "She came into Farmen's on her own, saw me sitting at that table, and decided to join me. The rest you pretty well know."

She shook her head. "Not really. From the way you two were acting, I thought you were on a date."

Evan grimaced. "Vanessa Brown is a spoiled, self-centered young woman." He touched the tip of Lorna's nose and chuckled. "Besides, she's too young for someone as mature as me."

Lorna laughed and tilted her head

so she was looking Evan right in the eye. "In this life we don't always get second chances, but I'm asking for one now, Evan Bailey."

He smiled. "You've got it."

"I think it's time for you to meet my in-laws."

"I'd like that."

"And I don't care how poor you are either," she added, giving his hand a squeeze.

"What makes you think I'm poor?"

"You mean you're not?"

He shook his head. "Not filthy rich, but sure no pauper." He bent his head down to capture her lips in a kiss that evaporated any lingering doubts.

Lorna thought about the verse of scripture Ann had quoted her awhile back. *"Take delight in the Lord, and he will give you the desires of your heart."* Her senses reeled with the knowledge that regardless of whether she ever taught music or not, she had truly found her heart's desire in this man with the blueberry surprise.

# RECIPE FOR
# BLUEBERRY SURPRISE

1/3 cup butter

2/3 cup honey

2 eggs

2 ripe bananas, mashed

1 1/4 cups all-purpose flour

2 teaspoons baking powder

1/2 teaspoon salt

1/4 teaspoon baking soda

1 cup blueberries

Cream butter and honey until fluffy. Add eggs one at a time, beating well after each addition. Add bananas and mix well. Combine dry ingredients and add to creamed mixture, mixing thoroughly. Gently fold in blueberries. Pour into 9×5-inch loaf pan lined with waxed paper. Bake at 350 degrees for 50 to 60 minutes or until wooden toothpick comes out clean. Cool, remove from pan, and gently pull away waxed paper. (Makes 1 loaf.)

# ABOUT THE AUTHOR

**Wanda E. Brunstetter** is a bestselling author who enjoys writing Amish-themed as well as contemporary and historical novels. Descended from Anabaptists herself, Wanda became deeply interested in the Plain People when she married her husband, Richard, who grew up in a Mennonite church in Pennsylvania. Wanda and her husband live in Washington State but take every opportunity to visit their Amish friends in various communities across the country, gathering further information about the Amish way of life.

Wanda and her husband have two grown children and six grand-children. In her spare time, Wanda enjoys photography, ventriloquism, gardening, reading, stamping, and having fun with her family.

In addition to her novels, Wanda has written Amish cookbooks, Amish devotionals, and several Amish chil-dren's books as well as numerous novellas, stories, articles, poems, and puppet scripts.

Visit Wanda's website at www .wandabrunstetter.com and feel free to e-mail her at wanda@wanda brunstetter.com.

The employees of Thorndike Press hope you have enjoyed this Large Print book. All our Thorndike, Wheeler, and Kennebec Large Print titles are designed for easy reading, and all our books are made to last. Other Thorndike Press Large Print books are available at your library, through selected bookstores, or directly from us.

For information about titles, please call:
  (800) 223-1244

or visit our Web site at:
  http://gale.cengage.com/thorndike

To share your comments, please write:
  Publisher
  Thorndike Press
  10 Water St., Suite 310
  Waterville, ME 04901